THE TRIP TO 1
SOMETHING VERY DIFFERENT . . .

Jerry and Joanne planned a nice, quiet golf outing in Arizona. Along the way they heard about the legend of the Lost Dutchman Mine and decided to go exploring in the Superstition Mountains.

It was the biggest mistake of their lives . . .

Searching For Jacob Waltz

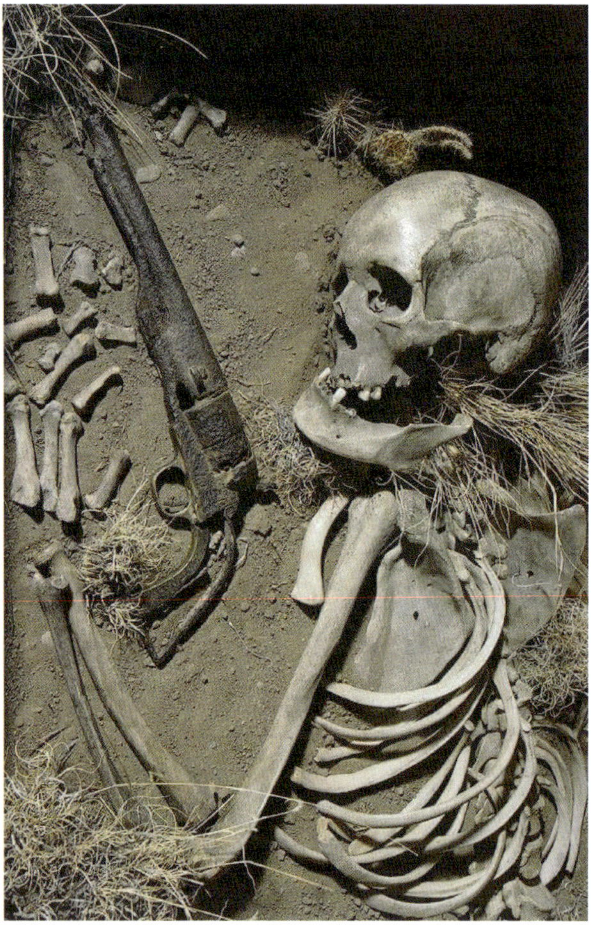

Searching For Jacob Waltz

Jim Redman

Copyright © 2016 by Jim Redman.

All rights reserved. Except as provided by U.S. and international copyright laws, no part of this publication may be reproduced, stored in a retrieval system or transmitted in any form or by any means without the prior written permission of the author, except for use of brief quotations in a review or journal.

This is a work of fiction. Names, characters, business establishments, places, events and incidents are either products of the author's imagination or used in a fictitious manner for literary effect. Any resemblance to actual persons, living or dead, or to actual events is purely coincidental.

ISBN: 978-1539455646

DEDICATION

To Arizona, the last of the contiguous states to join the Union and at once beautiful, beguiling, fascinating and - at times in certain places - hostile, dangerous and unforgiving.

CONTENTS

	Introduction	xi
1	The Vacation	15
2	The Boys	21
3	The Mountains	27
4	The Legend	31
5	The Stone Maps	35
6	The Hermit	39
7	The Plan	43
8	The Rendezvous	49
9	The Fork In The Road	53
10	The Superstitions	59
11	The Canyon	63
12	The Mine	69
13	The Interview	73
14	The Reckoning	83
15	The Night Shadows	87
	The Author	93

And there is no greater disaster than greed.

– Lao-tzu

INTRODUCTION

This is a work of fiction, although Jacob Waltz did live and many believe legends about him and the Lost Dutchman Mine have a basis in fact. The Superstition Mountains are real.

A word about the narrative settings and sources –
The *Fairmont Princess* is a well-managed premier destination resort in Scottsdale Arizona.

The *Rusty Spur* is a well-known Scottsdale western bar and restaurant, popular with locals and tourists alike.

There are many sources of information about Jacob Waltz, the Lost Dutchman Mine and the Superstition Mountains. The best overviews can be found in a number of articles on Wikipedia. More detailed information and history on the legend, and especially the Peralta Stones, can be found in excellent pieces by the late Jim Hatt on the website www.desertusa.com. This site is also a very good source for information about desert flora and fauna, including Javelina. Another fascinating overview of the legend is by Patrick Bernauw, at www.unexplained-mysteries.com. The author is indebted to these and to all others whose work has been helpful in framing the narrative storyline.

All photographs used are either sourced from Wikimedia Commons in the public domain, or have been circulated on social media without attribution.

The illustrations of old prospectors are by Alfredo Rodriquez, whose superb portrayals of old west figures, including Native Americans, are unmatched in detail and composition. His gallery can be accessed at www.alfredoartist.com.

The maps are from collections found at the Apache Junction Public Library, www.ajpl.org.

The painting of the skull at the end of Chapter 15 is by Giovanni Bellini, 1480, titled *Saint Francis in the Desert*.

Jim Redman
October 2016
email: jim@desertresources.com

1

The Vacation

JERRY KRANTZ LOVED THE ROAR of the Lamborghini exhaust as he pressed the accelerator down hard climbing the grade on the Interstate out of Indio. Next stop was Chiriaco Summit, the half-way point between Los Angeles and the Arizona state line.

He seemed a little lost in thought.

"What's on your mind Jerry?" Joanne asked.

"Just thinking about Max. He passed away just before we left. You remember him?"

"Of course. Maximilian Kupperman – the no-nonsense old codger with all the answers," said Joanne smiling.

"He *did* have all the answers – all the time. And a good thing for us he did. If it wasn't for him the company would have gone down the tubes instead of being brought back to life and made profitable enough to be sold. The whole family has him to thank for that."

"You're sure right about that Jerry. I wonder what your sister and her kids are doing with their share of the proceeds. Hope they aren't blowing it on expensive toys like this," said Joanne with a hint of sarcasm. Then continuing, "honestly Jerry you're like a teenager with his first hot car. Let's please not get a ticket before we're even out of California," she pleaded. "And another thing - wouldn't an ordinary SUV have been a more practical choice than this Italian status symbol that cost twice as much as our first house?"

"Hey honey, even after paying the rest of the family their shares, this baby cost only part of what we netted from the sale of the company, so why not? A car like this has been a dream of mine for a long time. Only go around once right? There's a time for practical and a time for fun. Besides, it's not like the Griswolds' in the movie *Vacation* -

no kids, no pets, no Aunt Edna, just us and golf clubs."

"I just worry about your tendency to . . . shall we say kind of flaunt it. Always the best that money can buy. Who else goes driving through the desert wearing $900 Italian loafers?"

"C'mon Jo, gimme a break . . . your sequined sandals aren't exactly from Goodwill, are they? Anyway, we're staying at a five star resort in Scottsdale so gotta go with the jet set, right?"

Chiriaco Summit is a favorite stop for travelers on this long stretch of the Interstate through the Mojave Desert. Indeed it's about the only stop with good facilities between Indio in California and Blythe in Arizona. A special attraction is the Patton Museum with its comprehensive collection of World War II hardware and memorabilia. But military history was the last thing on Jerry's mind as he and Jo finished their Dairy Queen cones.

"I cannot freakin' believe it . . . 85 in a 70 zone. The CHP must have nothing better to do than spoil a nice couple's weekend! And no 'I told you so' please!"

"Ok Jerry, I won't. But remember the officer clocked you at over 90 and could have lifted your license instead of just giving you a ticket if he wanted to. Then where would we be?"

"All I know is where we are now is running late

because of this idiot with a badge and gun throwing his weight around."

Joanne thinking to herself: *Yeah great, more immature behavior blaming somebody else... please God let's just get there and back home in one piece.* "Ok, Jerry could we just move on now please? How long before we get to Scottsdale?"

"Should be about 5 hours. And I promise to keep it under 100."

"Hey real nice car mister, is that a Ferrari?" the Circle K clerk seemed genuinely interested.

"Lamborghini. Don't you see any others like it here in Scottsdale?"

"I guess - not real sure. You folks staying here?"

"Yeah, little golf outing at the Princess. Can you give me directions from where we are? The dash GPS navigation screen went out during the drive."

"Sure, real easy. And you'll love it there. Kinda pricey, but the only way to go if you can afford it . . . "

"Yeah. Well thanks for the help," Jerry smiled as he handed the clerk two twenty dollar bills.

The clerk pocketed the $40 tip as he dialed the valet desk at the Princess. "Conley? It's Jason. Hey look for a California hotshot driving a brand new Lamborghini.

Should be checking in soon with a nice looking babe. This is a guy to get real close to. Got gas at the store, bought a few things and flashed a wad that could choke a horse."

"Mr. and Mrs. Krantz? Welcome to the Princess," Conley Wilkes showed his best smile. "We were expecting you some earlier - hope you didn't have any trouble along the way."

"Just glad to be here now, and looking forward to a relaxing few days."

"Let's get you checked in so you two can start relaxing starting right now. I'll take your clubs to the pro shop and then bring the luggage up to your room. If there is anything at all you'll be needing, I'll take care of it. Oh, and I'll make sure this beautiful car of yours gets parked where nobody gets close to it."

"Hey thanks - what was the name again, Conley? Right, sure appreciate it."

"One more thing Mr. Krantz - you'll be needing a good caddy while you're here. My cousin Tyler knows the course and everything else around here like the back of his hand. I'll make sure he's available for you."

"For crying out loud Jerry, I'd hate to nag but tipping this guy $100 bucks for carrying a couple of bags?"

"Look Jo, let me handle all this, ok? I know what I'm doing. You always want to get in with a savvy local at the front end when staying at a resort like this. Well worth slipping them a few bucks ."

"Yeah, maybe. I just hope your new best buddy isn't really more of a local redneck yahoo. When the sleeve of the valet uniform moved up - did you noticed his arm covered with tattoos?"

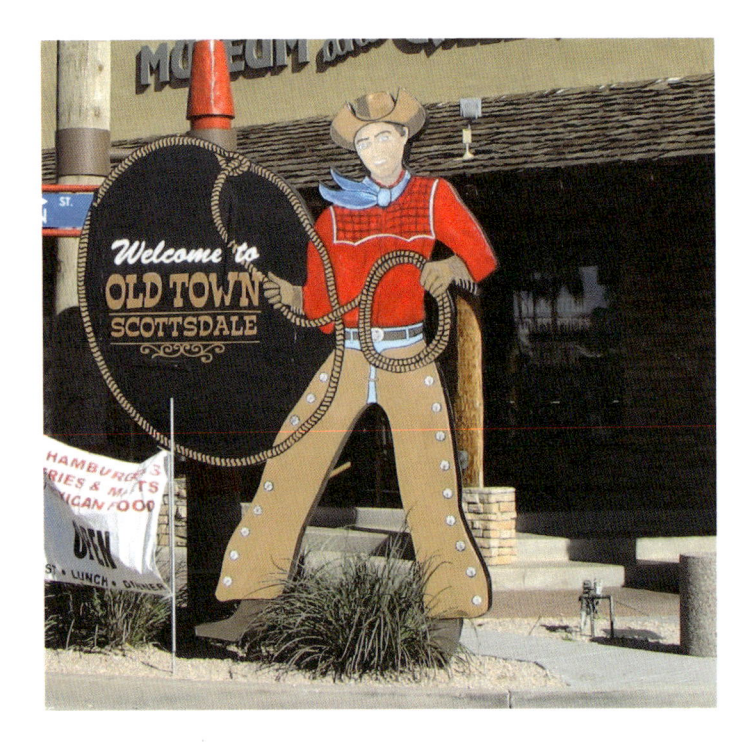

2

The Boys

SCOTTSDALE IS AN INTERESTING place demographically. It has a lot of ROG's - Rich Old Geezers, but also a fair number of millennials who party hardy at the bars, especially on Friday nights. And there's another large element - legions of service workers in food and hospitality, landscapers, housemaids, retail clerks, mechanics, and handymen doing chores the ROG's can't do for themselves. Also numerous are the professionals - medical, legal, accounting and financial advisory; all what you would expect in a community with both a high median age and wealth.

Then there are the criminals, actual or would-be. And hustlers hanging at the bars trying to score sex, drugs, money - or all three.

The *Rusty Spur* is not exactly front and center in the main tourist zone. But it's a long-time popular, sometimes rowdy, cowboy bar and the favorite place for Jason, Conley and Tyler to hang. Besides tourists looking for a lot of local color, regular patrons are the usual aging rodeo queens with bleached hair and very heavy makeup, and grandfatherly lounge lizards who spend nearly all day, every day telling each other the same war stories. All wear the obligatory cowboy hats and boots - all except Jason, Conley and Tyler, who preferred baseball caps with Nascar or National Rifle Association logos. Other regulars, buddies of Conley and his pals, were a tow truck driver and lot boy who worked at a local luxury car dealer.

"Jesus, a Lamborghini? No shit?" Lyle the lot boy was impressed, even though he washed dozens of nice cars every day. "Gotta be a hundred grand at least."

"Try way over four hundred grand," driver Dave chimed in. "Expensive mothers to buy, expensive mothers to own. So Conley, who is this dude?"

"Some asshole from Newport Beach," Conley responded. "The desk clerk got the whole skinny from the guy's travel agent. The dude inherited a business that just got sold. Typical spoiled California dipshit, you know the type. Really funny you know?"

"What's funny?" asked Dave.

"These idiots come to these five-star places, can't see through how we suck up to them, and haven't a clue that we know everything - and I mean *everything* about their lives. Just ask any of the maids . . . "

Another round of drinks and Dave is back to the Lamborghini. "You know it's kinda weird - you guys know Ricardo right? He was in here the other day and asked me about finding a real nice car that could maybe be boosted or chopped."

"Why would a small time dealer like him want to make a splash like that for?" Conley asked.

"Not for him. His weed and crack source down south

is a real Senor Big, they call him Don Carlos - who loves his toys, he's the one who put the word out. Ricardo said the guy would pay at least half of blue book for the right set of exotic wheels, plus delivery expenses."

"Can a Lamborghini be chopped Dave?" asked Conley, intrigued.

"Not easy but doable," Dave answered. "A car worth 400 grand has VIN's and micro chips hidden all over - engine, tranny, driveline, suspension, body parts, interior, glass, the works. No local shop could change them - but there are a few in Nogales who could. And it's so easy to get the Mexican Federales to look the other way. But no way would you chop this baby for parts, worth far more as a showy ride for a dude on a big ego trip. Just need to deal with the visible VIN's so it can be titled in Mexico. Of course there will be the old mordida for everyone involved down south," Dave added.

Conley was thinking out loud. "So this car is almost brand new, just needs the GPS fixed. So let's say current book is maybe $400 - $450,000...half of that is $200,000 on the low side - 40 grand each." Now looking smug and satisfied, turning to Dave, "talk to Ricardo and see if he can make a deal on the other end with Senor Grande and let me know what he says. Make it plain it'll be cash on delivery somewhere around here, the rest is strictly on him. I'll start thinking about how this might work. In the meantime Tyler, get your ass going early tomorrow. You have a golf date with this jerk off. Remember, play it sweet, suck up to him real nice and he should be good for at least a couple of c-notes tip."

3

The Mountains

JERRY SWUNG HIS CLUB like a weedwacker through the desert scrub with a vengeance.

"Any sign of it Mr. Krantz?" asked Tyler, trying hard to be helpful.

"I've seen rough before, but this is ridiculous," Jerry answered. "How many lost balls is that now?"

"Eight on the front nine. You might not want to poke around too much in that scrub - could stir up some nasty critters."

"Ok, let's pack it in," said Jerry. "I'm ready for a couple of cool ones in the clubhouse. You good with that?"

"You're the boss Mr. Krantz, whatever you say. We

just want our guests to enjoy themselves around here. As I'm sure Conley told you, taking total care of the guests is our number one job . . . "

"Yeah, Tyler, I feel like I'm in really good hands between you and Conley. Let's have that drink . . . "

"Great view from the deck here, Tyler - what are we looking at?

"It's some ways off but those are the famous Superstition Mountains."

"Pretty impressive, Tyler. Jo would sure appreciate that view," said Jerry. "Famous for what?"

"Ever hear of the Lost Dutchman Mine - Jacob Waltz?"

"Nope, remember I'm just an ex-surfer from Southern

California."

"Well, that's the old legend about gold, Spanish treasure and stuff - everybody around here knows some about it. Lot of people have gone up there following clues, searching . . . and not ever come back."

"You're shitting me! I gotta tell Jo, she loves stuff like this!"

"Tell you what Mr. Krantz, I'm pretty sure they have some books about the legend and the whole history in the gift shop. You and your wife might be interested in taking a look through them."

"May I help you?" Amber displayed the same gracious smile shared by all the resort staff.

Perfect teeth, nails, complexion, no botox, real nice little bod, thought Jerry, *wonder where they find all these chippies around here . . .*

"Amber? Tyler said to ask you about those mountains in the distance - said there might be books about old legends."

"Oh, the Superstitions . . . yeah they *are* something aren't they?" said Amber, again smiling. "Depending on the time of day either real pretty or kinda scary. They're part of a big wilderness park or preserve or something. You can get there going through Apache Junction."

"What about that lost mine?" Jerry asked.

"Yeah, the Lost Dutchman. I know people have been going up there searching for treasure for years and years."

"How about you Amber?"

"Lord no! My brother and his friends have though, mostly to hunt for Javelina. Seriously, it's totally too wild and remote for me, and no cell phone signal. Besides . . . "

"Besides what?"

"A girl could break a fingernail climbing around the rocks," smiled Miss Perfect Teeth.

"Jo look what I've got here."

"Why so excited Jerry? Did you break 100 on the course earlier?"

"Forget golf, I picked up a couple of books in the gift shop that you'll really be interested in."

"About what?"

"You know how you enjoy *Unsolved Mysteries* and shows like that? Well I just heard about a lost treasure up in those mountains off to the east. Hard to explain, but this really grabs me. Let's order dinner from room service while we look through this stuff . . . "

4

The Legend

JO FINALLY LAID HER book aside. "How's the one with the maps?"

"Fascinating. You know I prefer looking at pictures to doing a lot of reading. Looks like you're pretty into yours too."

"Jerry this whole story is just amazing - actually several stories woven together. Let me tell you what I found so far."

"The story begins way back when one MIGUEL PERALTA discovered a fabulously rich gold mine somewhere in the Superstitions. His family started mining the gold but were attacked and massacred by Apaches about 1850.

"Years later, a DR. THORNE treats an ailing or wounded Apache chief who rewards him with a trip to a rich gold mine. He is blindfolded, taken there by a circuitous route and allowed to take as much gold as he carry out with him before being escorted blindfolded out of the mountains. Thorne was unable or unwilling to ever go back to the mine, but about 1858 related his story to several U.S. Army soldiers stationed in the area. They went into the mountains to try and find the mine but never came back. Thorne's heirs reportedly still have some of the nuggets he kept.

"Now we come to JACOB WALTZ, a German immigrant born about 1810 - the 'Dutchman'. This was a common term for

THE LEGEND

a German in America since the words 'Deutsch' and 'Dutch' have a similar pronunciation.

"By around 1870 Waltz had settled in the Phoenix area and partnered up with another German, named WEISER. Together, these men while exploring the Superstitions, wind up rescuing a member of the original Peralta family, and are rewarded by being told the location of the mine.

"Later, while in the mountains Waltz and Weiser are both attacked by Apaches. Weiser survives only long enough to tell a DR. WALKER about the mine. Some time after, Waltz on his deathbed in 1891 relates the story of the mine to his nurse, a JULIA THOMAS and draws a crude map of the mine for her. Using the map, Thomas and a few acquaintances attempt to locate the mine. They are unsuccessful and eventually pass out of history.

"The legend of the LOST DUTCHMAN'S MINE really came to prominence in the summer of 1931 with the mysterious death of ADOLPH RUTH. Ruth, an amateur explorer and treasure hunter disappeared while searching for the mine. His skull was found six months later with two bullet holes in it.

"Ruth had first heard of the mine from his son, ERWIN C. RUTH who in turn had learned about it around 1912. It seems Erwin gave some legal advice to a PEDRO GONZALES that saved him from going to prison. Gonzales, who was descended from the original Peralta family on his mother's side, told Erwin about the mine and gave him some very old maps in gratitude for Erwin's help. Erwin passed on the information and maps to his *father Adolph who later began his tragic search.*

"In January 1932, six moths after his skull was found, Ruth's remains were discovered. Although scavengers had scattered the bones, his pistol and other personal items were recovered. The maps were missing. Among his effects was a note written by Ruth wherein he claimed to have found the mine. The note ended with the Latin phrase 'Veni, vidi, vice' - 'I came, I saw, I conquered'.

"Now closer to the present day, we have more deaths and disappearances. In the mid 1940's prospector JAMES CRAVEY disappeared after setting out to find the Lost Dutchman's Mine. His headless body was found some time later. In late 2009, a camper named JESSE CAPEN went missing after setting up camp in the Tonto National Forest on the edge of the Superstitions. His campsite and car were found abandoned and, three years later, his body discovered wedged in a crevice. In July 2010, Utah hikers CURTIS MERWORTH, ARDEAN CHARLES and MALCOLM MEEKS went into the Superstitions looking for the mine. In January 2011 three sets of remains believed to be those of the missing men were recovered."

"Wow Jo! Just wow - is all I can say. That, and what I've got here about the Peralta Stones and the maps make the whole thing just so fantastic. Check this out . . . "

5

The Stone Maps

"In the late 1940's, TRAVIS TUMLINSON, a police officer from Portland, Oregon was on a trip through Arizona. He stopped just outside Apache Junction to take a break and stumbled upon the corner of a strange stone sticking up out of the desert sand. What finally emerged was a set of three beautifully carved sandstone slabs, each about 18 inches wide, 12 inches high, and 2 inches thick.

"The slabs have symbols of a trail, a horse, a dagger and a priest. One has a recess for another heart-shaped stone that fits it exactly, and wavy lines that look like topographical features. The stones have collectively come to be known as the PERALTA STONE MAPS because the names 'Pedro' and 'Miguel' are *carved in them, both men spoken of in well-documented tales of*

The Priest Map

the original Peralta mining family. Jacob Waltz himself, on his deathbed years later, confirmed that his rich mine discovery was originally found by the Peraltas before they were massacred by Apaches.

The STONE CROSSES were found in 1983 by a miner named MICHAEL BILBREY, who was looking for indications of the lost mine. They were partially buried in loose gravel in a remote area of towering cliffs and deep valleys. Each cross is about 12 inches high, 6 inches wide, and an inch thick. Both crosses have engravings on one side. On one cross are words in Spanish, on the other are map-like symbols similar to those on the Peralta Stones, and the image of a heart. The crosses fit exactly within the outline of the cross carved into the surface of one of the slabs.

"The LATIN HEART is thought to be the most important part of the puzzle. Tumlinson, who discovered the stone slabs, returned to the area repeatedly to see if he could find any other artifacts. He had help searching by two local men, CHARLIE MILLER and BILL HINTON. Tumlinson finally gave up, but over a number of years Miller and Hinton continued searching and eventually, at the bottom of an old mine shaft found the Latin Heart.

"The Heart fits exactly into a matching recess that bears the date '1847' in one of the slabs. On one side of the heart are *inscribed a series of Latin words. The other side is covered with symbols that appear to be Roman numerals.*

The Heart Map

"Researchers believe the way to solve the mystery of finding the treasure is to follow the directions engraved on the slabs until you reach the end of the trail. Then you insert the heart into the cavity and the lines will point to the specific location. The problem is the directions on the slabs are so complicated and difficult to decipher that to date no one has been able to do it."

"Oh boy, Jo - what do you think now?"

"I think, Jerry, we've got to go up there before heading back home . . . "

6

The Hermit

CONLEY WAS DUE to go on his break and meet them. Jerry and Joanne fiddled with their coffee cups while waiting for him.

"You know Jo, I guess the whole legend could just be a hoax," Jerry mused.

"Of course it could," said Joanne. "Except for a few things - the Peraltas, Waltz and all the others are real – they lived and they died. The Apache massacre happened. The strange disappearances took place. The actual stone maps can be seen today in a museum and have been carbon-14 dated to the 1800's. But you know what most of all?"

"What's that?" asked Jerry.

"Nobody made any money off it like they would have if it really was a hoax."

"Mr. and Mrs. Krantz, sorry I'm a little late. Had to get a couple of guests checked in. How you folks doing?"

"Conley, make it Jerry and Joanne, ok? Reason we wanted to get together was the Lost Dutchman legend. You know Tyler saw I was kinda interested during our round yesterday and suggested we read a couple of books that were in the gift shop."

"Right, Tyler mentioned that. Find it interesting?"

"Huh, let me put it this way. It was early morning before we stopped reading and finally turned the light out. So Conley, you're from around here - what do you think about the whole story?"

"You know Jerry, I guess the feeling most locals have is there's something to it. There's too much recorded history for there not to be. I've been up there myself a number of times, mostly hunting and poking around. Definitely get some weird vibes from the old Superstition Mountains. Plus it's a fact people have died up there, some pretty gruesome. On the other hand, over the years a lot of people have gone in and come back out with no problems. As far as treasure, I personally think it's there somewhere yet to be found." Conley saw his opening. "You folks like to go take a look?"

"That's what we wanted to talk about. We're due to check out in few days. To be honest, I've kind of lost interest in any more golf. We don't have the clothes or gear to do any major exploring, but we'd like it if you could arrange for us to at least drive up for a quick look. It's really weird but both Jo and I feel drawn there somehow."

"I understand. Let me try to set something up so you might could meet Old Ben..."

"Who's that?"

"Old Ben is an old hermit prospector who's lived up there for many years. Some say he's what they used to call 'touched in the head', but I think he's harmless. When my buddies and I go into the mountains hunting, we always take him some food and a few supplies. In return he doesn't mess with our camp. It's funny, you can't find him - but he can always find you.

"But here's the thing you might really find interesting. You saw all the stuff in the book about the stones and the heart?"

"We did - how the Latin Heart points the way to the treasure . . . "

'Well, the legend says a little more - turns out another heart, more roughly carved out of rose quartz, sits right on top of the actual spot. Old Ben found that heart. He could show it to you."

7

The Plan

THE RUSTY SPUR WAS somewhat quiet, at least compared to normal. But it was after all only still late afternoon on a weekday. Noisy and rowdy would come a little later. This suited Conley, who wanted the full attention of his pals.

"Well looks like it's all coming together boys. The dude and his wife have give us the perfect opportunity - they're hooked on the Lost Dutchman Legend and want a little adventure in the Superstitions. So that's what they're gonna get . . .

"Here's want I kinda doped out. I'll set up a meeting at that old ranch off Peralta Road outside Apache Junction. They drive there in the Lambo, and Tyler and I will meet them in the four-wheel drive Explorer. They'll leave their car there, and then the four of us will drive up into the mountains to see if we can meet Old Ben, and get them even more stoked on the old legend, treasure and shit. While we're up there feeding them local color, their fancy car is gonna get stolen by wetbacks passing through."

"How the hell you gonna arrange that?" asked Dave.

"The wetbacks is you Dave. Can you make sure the dealership tow truck is available to go out to Apache Junction on a service call?"

"I guess . . . then what?"

"You load up the car and haul it from the old ranch out to Florence, " answered Conley.

"Why Florence?" Dave asked.

"Use your brains - no way can the car be seen around Scottsdale. Florence is perfect, just down the road from Apache Junction and the old ranch. Ricardo keeps a few of those ex-UHaul trucks there that he uses to bring dope and wetbacks across. The Lambo should fit in one of his vans no sweat. He's got the border fuzz on both sides on his payroll so it should be easy for him to make delivery to Senor Grande. But at that point we've got our money, cause it's cash on delivery baby."

"Hold on Conley - why even use the tow truck? I could just drive the car from the ranch to Florence."

"No way Dave. How you gonna explain it if you're stopped by fuzz along the way - what are you doing with the car and all that shit? But loaded on a legit tow truck with the driver in a uniform draws less attention. Cars aren't stolen that way. Plus your personal vehicle would be still be back at the ranch, so you'd have to get back from Florence somehow to get it. Too many chances for something to go wrong. This way you just drive the tow truck back to the dealership. when you're done. Right?"

Drinks all around. "What happens to the people Conley?" asked Jason.

"Not a thing," Conley answered. "If we do hook up with Old Ben, our nice couple from California will find him real interesting, maybe want to come back again for some serious treasure hunting. If Old Ben don't show they'll still love being up there seeing where the whole legend got started. Either way, of course they'll be major pissed when we get back to the ranch and see their car's gone. But no big disaster, Tyler and I take them back to the Princess and hold their hands while they get the insurance claim started and line up a rental car - you know, all those things we do for folks to help them out in their time of need. At the Princess we take real good care of our guests, right Tyler?"

"Yeah, right my ass - how you keeping a straight face Conley?" asked Jason sarcastically. "But here's my question - they gonna get in trouble with the insurance company, you know fraud or something?"

"Why Jason? They haven't done a thing - completely innocent. This dipshit has max insurance coverage so he won't even have a deductible, plus the rental car and all trip expenses back to Newport Beach are covered. I know because I checked his policy in the glove box."

"Won't the insurance company be suspicious, you know, wetbacks boosting a fancy car like that, all the alarms . . . ?"

Conley answered, smiling, "come on Jason, insurance companies in this part of the world know that these Mexicans can steal anything, anytime, from anywhere. They'll settle the claim and move on. Jerry and Joanne will be fine, we'll be fine, Senor Grande happy, everybody happy. This loss will be chump change to the insurance company - nobody hurt or killed, no lawsuits, no medical malpractice claims. Besides, like all insurance companies they're rolling in dough. We're just playing Robin Hood dudes - sharing the wealth from them that got it with them that can use it."

"Wait a minute - if Jerry takes his keys with him when he goes with you, how does Dave open the doors and start the car when he gets there with the tow truck?"

"The old fashioned way Jason - with the key. One of the side benefits of being a valet with a hotel concierge is I have custody of the keys to every car driven by every guest from the minute they check in until they leave. Not too hard to have a perfect copy made . . .

The Plan

"Jason, you and Lyle have to do something else. Tyler and I will be taking the couple up there in the Explorer. Dave will be handling the tow. Remember they are hoping to meet Old Ben. So you and Lyle need to drive up in your Jeep a few hours before we meet to see if he's around. And remember, ain't no cell phone service up there, so bring one of those short range two-way radio handsets that we take hunting. Only good inside a couple of miles but better than nothing. Tyler and I will have the other unit with us and give you a shout when we get near Weavers Needle. Likewise you call us when you hook up with Old Ben."

"I don't like it Conley - that crazy old coot gives me the creeps," said Jason anxiously.

"What you're gonna do Jason is take Ben some grub and booze. When we were up there a year or so ago, I told him we'd bring him some supplies next time. You know when we do that he acts real friendly and civilized like."

"What kind of grub?"

"Pick up two dozen big cans of cowboy caviar and a couple of bottles of that rotgut tequila from Alfredo's Market."

"Cowboy caviar - what the hell is that?"

"Jeez - you from around here and you don't know that Jason? Old cowboys and old miners, that's all they eat - plain old beans right out of the can . . ."

8

The Rendezvous

CONLEY HAD DECIDED it was best to meet Jerry and Joanne at the Starbucks down the street from the Princess. Not good to appear too chummy with guests on resort premises.

"Well folks, understand you're checking out day after tomorrow. I set things up for our little expedition in the morning. Only thing is, we need to start off in separate vehicles. Tyler and I will be coming in from Florence - have something to get set up down there before we hook up with you."

"Wait - you don't mean I have to drive up there in my car, do you?"

"No, no - we will meet at an old ranch that's just a few

miles from the trail up into the mountains. We'll leave your car there and then go together in Tyler's Explorer. It's four-wheel drive with good air conditioning.

"I also have asked another buddy to head up earlier in his Jeep and try to make sure Old Ben is around. That's really gonna add to the experience for you."

"Uh . . . ok, Conley if you think so. Just make sure you give me good directions to this ranch. If it's not part of the LA freeways I get lost pretty easy."

"No sweat Jerry, piece of cake. Did you bring that book with the old maps with you?"

"Yeah, there's a few reprinted in it - which one?"

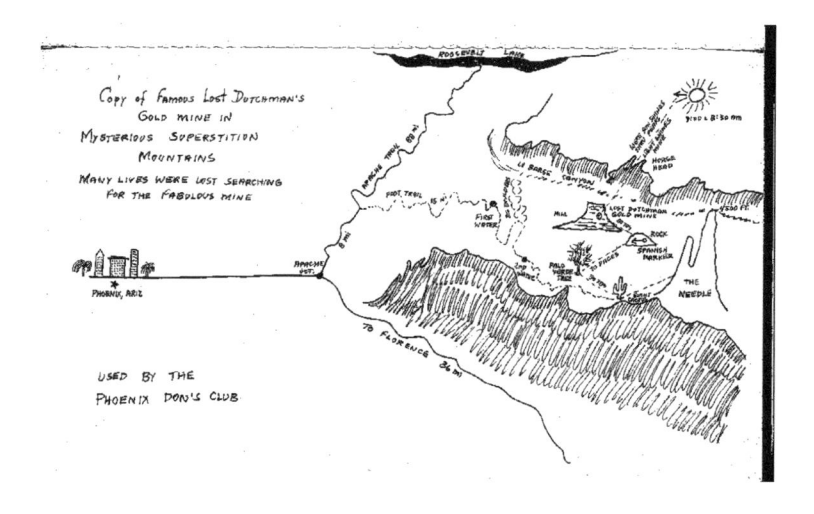

Copy of Famous Lost Dutchman's
Gold mine in
Mysterious Superstition
Mountains
Many lives were lost searching
for the fabulous mine

PHOENIX, ARIZ

USED BY THE
PHOENIX DON'S CLUB

"Ok, this one gives you an overview. Be nice if your GPS was working but no big deal. You see the main highway to Apache Junction? You take Apache Trail to the left, good paved road, travel 6 miles to what is marked here as a foot trail, then turn right. This map is old; that foot trail is now a pretty good road, paved for about 8 miles.

"Now this is important. Follow this road to where the pavement ends, then turn right onto a dirt road and go just a couple of miles to the ranch. That little stretch is dirt but in real good shape - we don't want you taking that nice car over anything rough. Park near the old barn. If we're not there before you we'll be along soon. Should take you about an hour from the hotel - say 10 in the morning?"

"You got it - this is exciting!"

"Great. Just remember - turn right where the pavement ends, you can't miss it."

9

The Fork In The Road

JERRY WAS GETTING NERVOUS, and trying hard not to show it. Jo stayed quiet, aware of her tendency to question his judgment, and fighting it.

Finally, he speaks. "This can't be right - this road is terrible. Didn't Conley say it was smooth dirt, just a couple of miles to that old ranch after the pavement ended?"

"He did. We must have bounced and crawled for miles now . . . "

"Yeah, and I turned left exactly at that spot - you saw the 'Pavement Ends' sign didn't you? Or were you dozing right then?"

"JERRY - HE SAID TURN RIGHT NOT LEFT!"

"Jesus, you're right, what a dumb shit . . ."

"MY GOD WHAT WAS THAT? SOUNDED LIKE A GUNSHOT! WHAT THE HELL?"

"JERRY!"

"Rear tire blown out honey. I can't freaking believe it - $600 top of the line Pirelli tires! At least we have full road hazard warranty on them . . . "
"Great - what difference does that make Jerry? What are you going to do, have the dealer in Newport send the VIP courtesy vehicle out?"

Back in the car. "I've never changed a tire before in my life but let me see what I can do. There's a jack and tire iron in the trunk with the spare. I think you need to loosen the lug nuts before jacking up the wheel. Here goes . . . "

"Jerry please that's enough - you're red in the face and getting overheated."

"Whew, just can't budge those nuts Jo. They must have gorillas tighten them at the factory. Let me stop and think for a few minutes . . ."

"We're in trouble Jo. Can't call AAA or anybody else for help, no cell phone service. We haven't seen another vehicle since turning off the Apache Trail. I guess Conley will come looking for us when we don't show at the ranch. But he may figure we went straight at that junction back there and headed on up into the mountains instead of doubling back. Lemme see that map book . . . "

"Looks like this whole area is covered with old trails, probably more for mules than vehicles. That's what we're on now. How much water do we have?" Jerry asked.

"Just those two bottles of Evian I took from the mini-bar back in the room." Jo answered.

"Not enough. We gotta decide - we could turn around and try to get back to the junction riding on the blown out tire - not sure how far we'll get. Or . . . "

"Look at this Jo. See that tall mountain on the map?

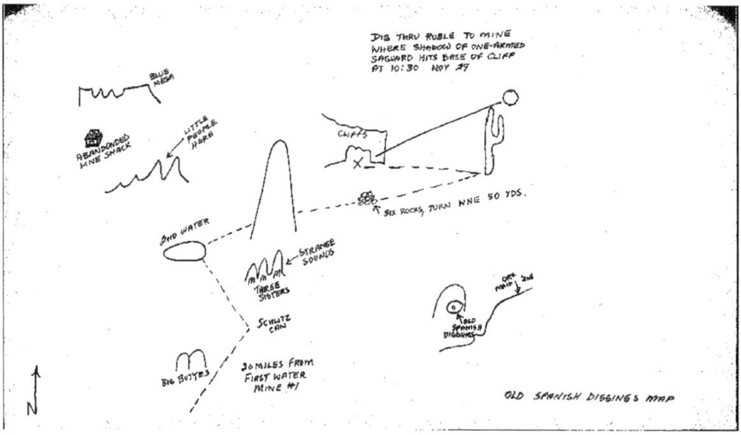
DIG THRU RUBLE TO MINE
WHERE SHADOW OF ONE-ARMED
SAGUARO HITS BASE OF CLIFF
AT 10:30 NOV
BLUE MESA
ABANDONDED
MNE SHACK
LITTLE PEOPLE HERE
CLIFFS
SIX ROCKS, TURN NNE 50 YDS.
2ND WATER
STRANGE SOUNDS
THREE SISTERS
SCHLITZ CAN
BIG BUTTES
20 MILES FROM
FIRST WATER
MINE #1
OLD SPANISH DIGGINGS
N
OLD SPANISH DIGGINGS MAP

"That's Weavers Needle, got to be - no other shape like it. And that's it up ahead, maybe 4 or 5 miles. We've got to have water - these old maps have x's marking water here and there. This trail we're on looks like it'll get us there . . . "

"What should we do - will the car last?" asked Jo, very worried.

"Better chance of getting up there than trying to make it back the way we came."

"Jerry . . . we're . . . not going to die are we?"

"Not without a fight Jo - a real fight . . ."

10

The Superstitions

CONLEY REALLY HATED it when things didn't go as planned. He sorted through the possibilities.

"How long we been waiting now Tyler?"

"Little over 45 minutes"

"Hmmm - ok, I'll stay here. You drive back to Apache Junction and call the Princess to see if they're still there. Then come straight back here. If they haven't left the hotel, guess they changed their mind about the whole thing. If they did leave, that dipshit must of gotten lost - and we gotta go find them."

The sound of the shredded tire flapping against the wheel well of the car finally stopped. It was replaced by a grinding sound.

"What's that noise Jerry?"

"Has to be something with the rear axle - bearing maybe, I don't know. Can't go forever riding on rims through sand and rocks. But we need to keep on pushing until it just quits and won't move. Any few feet closer to Weavers Needle is that much less to cover on foot."

"But your new car - we're gonna wreck it!"

"Screw the car - only our lives matter now . . . "

"So for sure they left the hotel early enough to make it

here at 10?" Conley asked.

"Yep," Tyler answered. "And Ashley at the front desk said they're still registered, haven't checked out. When Denny brought their car around, they told him they were just going on a little day trip."

"Tyler, my guess is they went straight instead of turning right to get to the ranch. Only way they could have gone - the old mule trail to the left is way too rough. So they gotta be up ahead, maybe even got up into Needle Canyon. Christ almighty, I hate to think what that idiot is doing to the car..."

"Should we have stayed with the car Jerry?"

"No Jo, there's no water around there. Anyone who spots the car and checks it will see the note on the dash and know we've come up this way. Hang in there Jo - I know it's hard." Smiling, "you were right about these Italian loafers - we both sure could have used some hiking boots. Next time we stop at the Sports Authority first, right?"

Jo smiling weakly, "right - if there is a next time..."

"I've got to rest Jerry, got to stop, please..."

"Sure honey. At least there's plenty of shade here in

the canyon. Drink some water from the last Evian bottle, finish it. I'll find us more someplace soon."

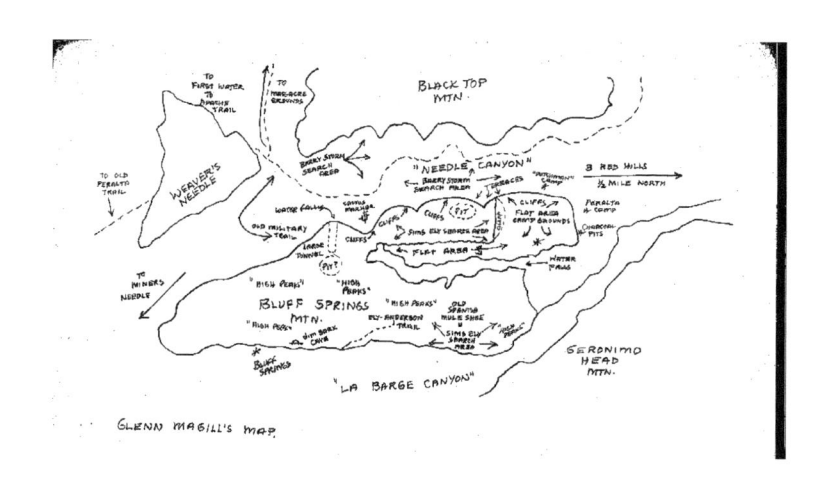

GLENN MAGILL'S MAP.

11

The Canyon

The two shots echoed from each side of the canyon walls.

"Jerry!"
"Those are gunshots - close! Get down Jo and stay down!"

"Hear anything at all?" Jo asked.
"Not since those shots. If they were shooting at us we would have heard or seen something. We can't stay behind this rock forever. The sun is starting to go down - I'm going to walk up the canyon a ways . . . " Jerry answered, now more feeling more confident.

Now from further up the canyon, Jerry called out, "come with me Jo, there's a jeep up ahead there – think it's safe, nobody around it."

The jeep had bounced over a boulder and was jammed up against one of the canyon walls. Both doors were wide open.

"Wonder what the hell is going on. Look at this – those are shell casings on the floor, and two holes through the side window . . . *shot from the inside!* No blood, just looks like whoever was in the jeep was surprised, or attacked or . . ."

"What's in the back seat Jerry?"

"Whoa - we're in luck. Two canteens at least half full. And - a cardboard box with cans of food and booze. Hold on - something else on the floor, looks like a small two-way radio."

"Turn it on , maybe we can reach somebody who can help."

A lot of static at first, then as Jerry changed channels on the handheld they heard a familiar voice:

"JASON, COME IN. JASON IT'S CONLEY - DO YOU READ ME? JASON, YOU IDIOT - TYLER AND ME ARE ALMOST UP TO NEEDLE CANYON. JASON? LISTEN THE PLAN HAS TURNED TO SHIT. NO SIGNS OF THE PEOPLE OR THE CAR. JASON? YOU HEAR ME? IF WE DON'T GET THAT CAR YOU AND LYLE CAN KISS YOU SHARES GOODBYE. JASON?"

Standing alongside the abandoned jeep, Jerry could barely contain his anger. *"Son of a bitch! Son of a god damned bitch! Bastard! I can't believe I let us be set up like that! Conley's a good name for the bastard, 'Con' is right!"*

"Jerry - what do we do now? From what we just heard on the radio he's headed up here!"

"Not sure. Sounds like they were gonna steal the car somehow. But killing us? How would they get away with that?"

"Can we get out in this jeep"

"Keys are in the ignition, but it'll never move with the front wheel wedged between the boulder and the wall like that."

"Who were the guys in the jeep? What happened to the them?" Joanne asked.

"Had to be Conley's buddies who were supposed to come up first and find the old hermit prospector – remember, the one who found the carved heart . . . "

"Right - Old Ben . . .did he attack them?" asked Joanne.

"Had to be. Who else - Apaches? The driver got off a couple of shots but then . . ."

Joanne again, "is the gun in the jeep still?"

"No - not on the ground either. Could be in the rocks somewhere - but I don't want to waste time trying to find it," Jerry answered.

"Look Jo, we got to get to some kind of shelter quick. At least we have water now and can take some of these cans of beans with us. I can open the cans with the tire iron. Let's head up further into the canyon - looks like there's some crevasses and openings in the walls."

"Hey Jerry, I just was thinking - if it was Old Ben, why didn't he take the food . . . ?"

Tyler had parked the Explorer well back from the jeep. He approached from one side, Conley from the other.

"What the shit! It's jammed against the wall and front axle broken - why the hell are the doors wide open?" exclaimed Conley. "And look at the passenger window - it's shot out!"

"Conley - I got a real bad feeling about this. Let's go get some help."

"To do what? Have the law come back up here and question everybody they can find about what went down, with the car and all?"

"But what happened to Jason and Lyle? We gotta find them!" Tyler said.

"Slow down, slow down. Let's think about this. Check on the floor front and back . . ."

"These are 9mm shell casings. Didn't Jason have a gun like that?" asked Tyler.

"Yeah, Glock semi-automatic, and knew how to use it. With 10-shot magazine - why the hell only 2 shots? You see the gun anywhere?"

"Nope. Look here, looks like the food carton's been opened, 6 or 7 cans gone," said Tyler. "Old Ben must of finally flipped out and jumped them."

"Maybe, maybe. But I don't figure both Jason and Lyle getting surprised by one old man like that."

"So who else?"

"The dipshit and his wife. Maybe they made it here before us. Hey did you hear any shots as we were coming into the canyon?"

"No - but the four wheel drive in low range was making a lot of noise."

"See any tracks in the sand around the jeep?"

"Some. Not boots though, more like sandals and dress shoes."

"Tyler, we got some serious shit to deal with here. Somehow that couple made it up here and tangled with Jason and Lyle. Got to assume they got Jason's gun. Don't see the two-way handset either - must have that too. I never figured that spoiled California peckerhead for this kind of nerve, but I know one thing . . . "

"What Conley?"

"Only two people gonna get out of these mountains - and we're them standing right here. Sun's going down fast, let's get moving up the canyon. We got wheels - they're on foot, shouldn't take long . . . "

"You got your gun Conley?"

Patting the shoulder holster, "right here, near and dear to my heart - .357 magnum. Never leave home without it."

12

The Mine

THE OPENING WAS NEAR the top of the canyon wall, visible in the fading light from the bottom. It looked high enough to be able to stand in. Jerry saw there was also a pretty clear trail leading to the entrance.

"C'mon Jo, just a little higher - we're almost there. Then we can rest and be safe."

"Can this be the lost mine Jerry?"

"I don't know. Obviously it's been worked - look at these supports. More than one person, and over a pretty long period of time."

"How far back do you think it goes?"

"No idea. But we need to stay close to the entrance - no way of knowing what's way back in there. I can see back 50 feet or so, some loose boards and debris. Think I'll try to bring some of it up to the entrance while there's still a little light. Got to make some sort of a barricade."

"Hey Jo - there's some old rusty cans and trash back here. Looks like a campfire at some time too - somebody's been living in here . . . "

"Still see those tracks Tyler?"

"Yeah, but light is almost gone. For sure there's only two of them, one set look like that flat sandal type."

"That's the babe. But where the hell are Jason and Lyle?"

The Mine

―――――

"Jo, give me a hand if you can. I want to push this old timber under a couple of these small boulders and roll them into the entrance."

"Ok. Hey - Jerry? Did you hear anything just now way back in there?"

"Like what?"

"I'm not sure, like squeaking or . . . maybe chattering?"

―――――

"Tracks going up this old trail. Where's it lead Conley?"

"Don't know Tyler. We been in the canyon before but I don't reminder this trail angling up the wall. Can we go up in four wheel low?"

"Think so. But I got to turn the big lights on and take it real slow so's we don't go over the edge . . . "

―――――

"Jerry! They're all around us!"

"Bats! Cover your head and eyes! That's the

chirping you heard a little while ago. There's thousands of them! All heading out of the entrance for the night!"

―――――

"Tyler - you see that opening up there?"

The light from the overhead high beam on the truck rack illuminated the old mine portal. "They've got to be in there. Switch off the engine and lights Tyler, rest of the way on foot. Let's get go. . .”

"Wait - what the hell is that? Tyler? Tyler! . . ."

―――――

"Jerry! I just saw a light down there! Was real bright shining toward us - then went out. - now there's noises! Something's happening!"

"Jo! They're Right outside the entrance! Footsteps - grunts - what's that smell? Jo! get behind me - now . . . ! "

13

The Interview

Jerry glanced around the room, noticing little things - the ceiling fan, metal desks and chairs, the nameplate on the desk in front of him:

Sgt. R. L. 'Buck' Rogers, Chief Deputy

"We want you folks to be comfortable - you both been through quite a lot. Care for any coffee or water?" asked Rogers.
"Water for me," Jerry responded. "How about you Jo?"
"Same, thanks."

"Ok," Rogers continued, "I want to introduce Randy Hoskins here. He's the Supervising Ranger for the Tonto National Forest - that's the agency that oversees the area up there where you were found. We'll be joined by a couple of others here shortly - the county Sheriff himself and an investigator from the state CID. Also, there will be a stenographer present. We're gonna wait for them to get here before taking formal statements, but we can talk some before then. Any questions?"

"How exactly did you find us? asked Jerry. "The paramedics didn't say much - and if they did we were both kind of out of it."

"I'm damn sure you were! Lucky no real injuries. You'll both have to stay off your feet for a while - especially you Mrs. Krantz. Some pretty bad cuts and blisters you got there.

"Anyway," Rogers went on, "a Forest Service helicopter spotted your car, obviously stuck on that trail a few miles below Needle Canyon, and abandoned. When they broadcasted the description, Scottsdale police came back saying the Princess reported two guests missing overnight but still checked in. In the meantime, we had dispatched a couple of deputies to go out to the car in a 4x4. They found your note which was a big help.

"Then it got interesting. The hotel also reported two employees who didn't show up for work as scheduled for the morning shift - the Wilkes cousins, Conley and Tyler. Did you know them?"

"Yeah, unfortunately," Jerry answered. "Kind of a long story . . . "

"Hold that part for a bit, we're gonna want to hear a lot more about that.

"Our department and Forest Service then set up a coordinated search with our two choppers. That's when we found two more vehicles up in Needle Canyon. You know about those?" asked Rogers.

"Yes, we saw the jeep and . . . "

"Mr. Krantz, probably need to stop you now. You

know, this is an informal interview to try and tie up some loose ends - for your sake and ours. I'm sure you want to know a lot more about what went down, just like we do. You familiar with Miranda rights?"

"Like when people are arrested?"

"That's it. You folks aren't under arrest right now, but we do have five missing."

"What! *Five*? Who?"

"Coming to that. But first I have to advise you of your rights. They're spelled out on this card. If you want an attorney, we'll suspend the interview until you have one present. If you're ok with continuing, both of you need to sign the waiver on the back of each card."

"Sure, you bet - we got nothing to hide. Right Jo?"

"So Sergeant Rogers, tell us please! Who's missing?"

"Let's start with the tow truck driver from Millennial Motors in Scottsdale, Dave Renfro. First question is - how did you call him without cell phone service out there?"

"What? What are you talking about? We never called for any tow truck - don't know about any car dealer in Scottsdale. You say he's missing?"

"Yep, there's an old deserted ranch off Peralta Road out of Apache Junction. Looks like he started out from there and headed out to where you folks turned off the paved road. That's where we found the tow truck. It was still in running condition, so why he left it and where he went is a mystery. There were other recent vehicle tracks close by so he may have been picked up by someone else. But judging from some oil stains in the sand, it looks like the truck was parked for sometime at the ranch before heading off to the junction where you made the wrong turn. The real funny thing though – both he and somebody else from the car dealer didn't show up to work this morning . . . a young kid named Lyle who detailed cars. But the folks at the dealership said Dave drove off in the tow truck by himself. What do you make of all that Mr. Krantz?"

"Holy shit . . . I . . . I just don't know what to say. What about the other vehicles, the jeep and the one we saw when the chopper picked us up at the mine?"

"The jeep was registered to Jason Morris. He worked at the Circle K on Scottsdale Road near the Princess. We found shell casings on the floor of the jeep, and cans of food and booze in the back. Big thing though - looks like shots were fired from inside the vehicle, that shattered the passenger window. The other vehicle, the Ford Explorer was down the trail from the mine entrance where you two holed up. It was registered to Tyler Wilkes, and we think probably Conley was with him. There was a loaded .357 magnum on the floor, unfired. Both the jeep and the Explorer were sitting with the doors wide open. No signs of the men. I can tell you Morris and the Wilkes cousins all had done some prison time. We also know that the Wilkes cousins, Jason, Dave and Lyle were more or less good buddies who hung together. I think you know now why we're treating this as criminal activity. How about you tell us all you know about this situation?"

"Well, that's about it Sergeant," said Jerry soberly, "the whole story. You want to add anything honey?"

"Just that there was something about this Conley that made me nervous - from the first day when we checked in," Jo offered.

"I'm not surprised," said Rogers. "His rap sheet shows priors for identity theft and involvement in a luxury car theft ring. Something about him - he's not the typical redneck lowlife. He comes out of that background, but we think he always fancied himself able to hang with better class folks - like yourselves. Working at a 5-star resort suits him perfectly. He's very smooth and a charmer, probably charmed the personnel manager every place he's ever worked. Also, his past criminal activity indicates he kind of acts like the mastermind and gets somebody else to do the dirty work."

"I call him a phony, son of a bitching bastard - pardon my French Sergeant . . . " said Jerry angrily.

"Can sure understand that Mr. Krantz. Let's take a

short break and then cover who you think was trying to get at you two in the mine."

Jo began. "It was absolutely terrifying. We knew from hearing the two-way radio that they were just behind us. Then, when those bats starting flying I almost passed out. Thank God Jerry kept his cool - and was able to pile up enough boards and rocks to keep anybody out of the mine. It worked too - they were just outside but couldn't get in."

"Who couldn't get in?"

"Well, I don't know - Conley and Tyler? and maybe the other two from the jeep. Sounded like a lot of movement right outside the entrance."

"Mr. Krantz? How do you see it?"

"Whoever was just outside the entrance was gone after about an hour - that doesn't sound like Conley giving up like that. And why would he leave his gun in the Explorer? I'm kinda back to thinking the old hermit prospector is behind it all - you know, Old Ben . . . "

Sergeant Rogers looked at Ranger Hoskins for quite a while before turning back to Jerry.

"We'll come back to Old Ben in a bit. First, I want to tell you who was outside the entrance. Remember the grunts and smell?"

"Yes, vividly!"

"We found the tracks of a Javelina herd all around the entrance. You know about them?"

"What are they? Do we have them in Newport Beach?"

"No, I don't think so! These are native to this part of the country, kind of like desert wild boar. They are active at night and can be dangerous, especially the males who have some mean tusks. They root around and eat just about anything, from cactus to snakes. The males also have scent glands that give off a distinctive odor. That's what you smelled."

"Mr. and Mrs. Krantz, the others should be here at any moment. Ranger Hoskins and I have taken notes, but I'm afraid you'll have to go through it again for the stenographer, and then sign your statements."

"Well, ok I guess. But why twice?"

Sergeant Rogers smiled. "You ever watch NYPD? You know why - we want to make sure the two versions of your story match.

"A few more details. You'll need to stay around for a few days in case we need anything else from you. But you'll be needing to arrange for transportation anyway. I guess you realize your nice car is probably totaled - looks like the frame's twisted and rear axle shot, plus other stuff. Those Italian status symbols just aren't made for off road travel . . . "

"That's alright Sergeant. We're gonna do what Jo wanted in the first place - buy the cheapest SUV we can find that doesn't attract any attention.

"Jo and I just got to ask you officers now - who do *you* think is behind the disappearances. Old Ben?"

"We know it's not Old Ben. You see, we found his remains all the way back in the old mine you were in.

"He's been dead for at least a year . . ."

14

The Reckoning

RICARDO NAVIGATED THE HUMMER very carefully between the narrow walls of the slot canyon.

"Ok, I think *Senior Dave*, the chopper no see us now,"

he said. *"Gracias a Dios!"*

"That's a break," Dave answered. "Hey amigo – what say you drop the greaser lingo and just speak American now? I know you can . . . "

"Sure Dave, *no es problema,*" said Ricardo, smiling broadly. "You know *amigo,* you one lucky *hombre* I come along and pick you up."

"For sure, you got that right. When I saw there was no car at the old ranch I knew that there was a major screw up – or, more likely Conley had crossed us. What made you come out to the ranch when you did?"

"*Mi* – how you say it – *seis,* 6 senses. When you no show up in Florence I figure you in trouble maybe."

"Good thinking Ricardo, I owe you one. Got to hand it to you – knowing the back way into Needle Canyon and these little slots, you sure know your way around the these mountains . . . "

"*Si – mis compadres y yo,* we be all through the canyons around here. Lots places to hide weed and crack from down south, for moving out to sell later. Only thing though . . . "

"What's that?"

"The spirits of *Los Viejos,* the Old Ones, all around, sometime angry, *muy peligroso* . . . "

Sounds of the chopper had long since faded.

"I'm thinking it's safe to start heading back out to Needle Canyon and get out of here before dark, what do you say Ricardo?"

"*Si*, and I've got to get the money back to Don Carlos in Nogales *pronto*. He will be pissed about what happened."

"Why? So he missed out on the car, there'll be another one down the road. And it's dirty money anyway – no harm, no foul right?"

"I think you *no comprende* how this business works *mi amigo*. *Numero ono*, the extra money for expenses already spent. *Numero dos*, you no get second chance in this game. But big thing, now the *dinero* in bag in trunk got to go back to Carlos *pronto!*"

"Ok, Ricardo, whatever you say," said Dave. Then changing the subject, "I wonder who got to the boys down the canyon. There were shots fired by somebody, and the doors open on both vehicles is real strange. Lot's of tracks, but no signs of them. We're lucky we got out of there before the chopper and the searchers arrived."

"*Si, es verdad* Dave. Wonder where is the car you think?

"Don't know. There was no sign of it from where I left the tow truck and the trails all around were way too rough for it. But regardless I blame Conley. Always so smart, all the answers, bossing the rest of us around."

"Well him not boss anymore. Maybe not good what

happen but he I think try for all the money, *verdad?*" Ricardo said.

Dave was trying to sort things through. "I guess we'll never know what really happened to those guys. But I wouldn't be surprised if Conley had set up an ambush to take us out. Funny, just like I was planning to do to him. Could be that couple from California surprised them . . . "

"*Cuatros hombres*? No, *Senior Dave* no way that *Californio* and his *mujer* take care of four men! It be the spirits up in these *montanas!*"

"Yeah, could be, who knows. Sure enough weird shit gone down around here for a long time. Anyway Ricardo, time for us to settle up."

"*Como* Dave? What you mean?"

Dave's gaze narrowed as he pulled the pistol from his waistband. "You know, Ricardo, split the money . . . "

"MADRE DE DIOS! MONEY FROM CARLOS FOR CAR! NO CAR NO MONEY!"

"Yeah, that was the old deal. The new deal is Dave gets to stop driving a tow truck for a living – so ADIOS RICARDO . . ."

15

The Night Shadows

The shadows of the spires and buttes first lengthen, then get shorter as the moon rises and light reaches the canyon floor.

Now life stirs.

The diamondback rattlesnake begins its sinuous crawl over rocks and sand, tongue flicking here and there. It knows it must finish its night hunt and return to shelter before the morning sun rises too high.

The first mournful howl of the coyote sounds, soon joined by a chorus of his fellows.

Further off, a cougar screams. Its jaw clamps on the mule deer's throat. The predator screams, the prey dies silently.

A flash across the moon face, but no sound. The Great Horned Owl glides noiselessly over the canyon floor, just missing the kangaroo rat that reaches its burrow.

The Javelina root around, finishing gnawing flesh off the skeletons of the four men. The shuffle of their many little feet cause the bones and the gun to get buried in the loose sand. The skulls are too large to get covered. Moonlight reflects on them as they roll to the side of the sandy wash. They won't be completely buried by wind and water for perhaps many seasons.

The soft tread of the Old One's moccasins makes almost no sound. But the Javelina pause, alert. Time to return to the cave. They stop and follow him obediently.

The mountains have seen and they have heard. The

mountains don't care, they just watch and listen. As it has been for a very long time.

And the mountains don't tell.

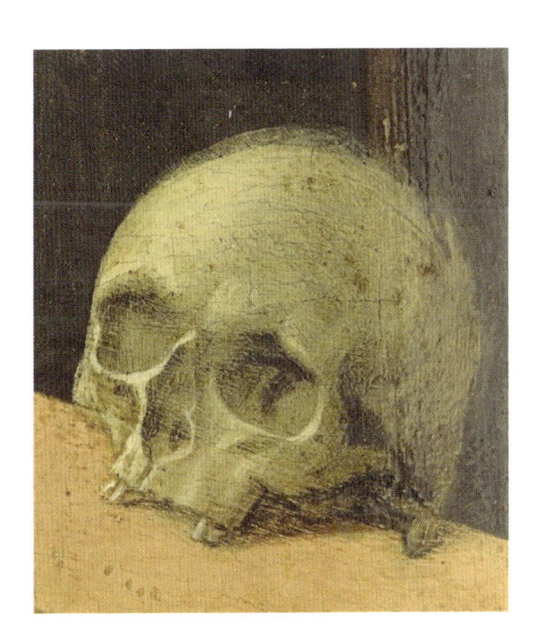

ABOUT THE AUTHOR

JIM REDMAN spent over 30 years living in California before semi-retiring to Arizona in 2004. During his professional career he served as CEO of a diversified industrial firm, and as CEO of a publicly traded company that did crisis management consulting for clients in various industries.

He is the author of *The World According to Max*, and divides his time now between client assignments, researching material for writing projects, and exploring the Sonoran Desert.

His family moved to the Phoenix area in the 1940's, and he first heard the story of Jacob Waltz from his parents who had ventured into the Superstitions briefly on a couple of occasions.

They never went back.

Searching For Jacob Waltz

Made in the USA
Charleston, SC
25 October 2016